BLACK PORTRAIT

i

BLACK

PORTRAIT

POEMS

SHORT STORIES

BY

THOMAS DECKER

iii

BLACK PORTRAIT

RED

Rage fills my cup

My fists

The blood in my paint

The words on the steel wall have tongues

Pink like a lovely dress

Sharp like a lover's glare

These steel halls are wet with red

These steel halls are red with dread

SUFFERERS PLEAD

This is where all the sufferers plead

Where no one tries to find what they need

Crowds are spread around a power source

But mice in the ground caution its deadly grasp

REAL

The crowds have had enough

No more laughs rising at dusk

Happiness can have selfish intentions

You must run away and find all interventions

PLAY A LITTLE SONG

I'm starving

You don't know me

The lights of the night are gone

Pitch black remains

Play a little song

And I'm starving

I don't know you

4

MELODY

Glory is on his last stand

Destiny is laughing in his own choir

Try to sing the melody

The wind will blow the castle down

So, turn away!

But try to fly inside!

Sing to me

Oh, dear Melody!

The sound's honor needs to return

Music sleeps in her hidden room

Kept away

EAGLES

Don't act like I don't miss you

The eagles still sit near my window

Their golden beaks razed the glass

My shotgun aimed

I screamed

"It's already done! Leave me be!"

The madness went on until I broke a mountain

A few weeks later I took down the papers

The pictures

The songs

I knew this would happen all along

With the treasures in the box

The eagles stopped coming

With the feathers in a jar

The crows stopped crowing

WALKING ALONE

Walking alone is something that keeps me sane

I'm not mad at you

Well, I guess I am

I want to sit in a tree

Is there something I can see?

Nope, no one is here

Shut up

Shut up

I'll clean the blood

Clean the knife

The deed is done

I'm not mad anymore

Well, I guess I am

Or maybe…

THEY CAN'T HEAR ME

Streets are lonely

Filled with people

They're so lonely

Well I'm not dead

My hands don't know

That my head knows of my shouts

And I don't know

My own streets

Are the ones with the dirty deeds

He doesn't know

That his actions

Will see the wind

But not the thrones

Well I guess he does

He doesn't care though

Manipulative voices

Are the only friends he meets

So, I walk the streets

Foreign or home

Only some feel great to me

The biggest group will always be

But never until the end

Voices grow

They don't know you

Not even your favorite sound

Or your ugliest roar

But they think they do

Special ones

9

They walk with me

I can't show the faces to them

Voices run inside

Lock themselves up

The special ones will never understand

The voices want it both ways

HEART

Out of hand

Out of air is my voice

Limbs have turned in their resignations

Out of smiles

Out of laughs are my eyes

Emotions leak shades of white upon darker white

Out of trust

hate fuels my skepticism

I'm walking past my pumping heart

I keep trudging through the street

I feel like I'm walking through the sun

EEL

When you hold my hand

Please tell me you'll see my ocean flow

It's filled with coral reefs

And growing parasites

The ocean is going through a storm

Tomorrow the sun will shine

The fish are in their homes

They never want to mess with the eel

I slither right through the sunlight

Tell me you'll slither with me too

The coral reef is green

Blue, red, and some pink

Mixed with spilled black

The clownfish have called my name

The fun and games led right to the sand

They never wanted to see the eel

I slither right through the moonlight

Tell me you'll slither with me too

REST IN PEACE

Boiling heat

Summer days

Nothing here my eyes can't see

Howling wind screaming through the day

But no one sings like you anymore

Fear the dead

Ask the wise

No one dares to try to spy

Living ghosts don't notice all the words that they clearly try to sing

Dig a hole

Make a home

Let it fill up more and more

Clearly you don't know of all the knocks at no one's door

CARE

Killing

"Talk to someone who actually cares about them"

Kneeling

"Grab two hands and fill them up with a smile"

Ignoring

"Everything is fine, don't look back!"

Fearing

Stars and laughs are what they want to see

Watching

"Witnessing is not what you should do!"

Grabbing

They want you to walk this way

MARKS

Find me on the floor above

The room above your eyes

The tumor has been turned black

Just like the marks on your back

Racing through the images

While you stand with the coldest stare

Sickness is half the pain

A muddy crystal ball is the other

SOFT SMILE

Red on white

High beauty and mellow

Soft smile please stay for a while

Tapping on doubt

Pretty words go South

Find a moment

Not this moment

Pretty words go North, South, East, and West

GOLD

Hands on the door

Fingerprints

Fingerprints

Lungs suspended on the ceiling

Birds are eating all the fried beans

Voices made of gold

Are what you sell to the kingdom

Voices of gold

Are the forked tongues that are shaking hands

20

ALONE

Don't leave me alone

Stories are too much to handle

"Today was great! We had so much fun!"

Staring at the wall and I'm in the dark

I know of laughs only I can hear

You don't need to be asleep to have nightmares

Chuckle

Hug

Squeeze

Don't leave me alone…

COLORS

Blue

Yellow

Green

Red

Colors that mix

Paint the neurons

Pink

Brown

White

Purple

Colors that grow

Feed the veins

Shake

Shake

Shake

22

Shake

I couldn't find the colors today

LOOK DOWN

The wind passes slow on my tired legs

"Walk alone or else"

The sun is shining

Every day the sun does that

"Look down"

I just want to go home

"Look down"

Dreams are my escape

"Look down"

My hand can only hold the air

Look down

"Walk alone or else"

FOREST

My forgiveness is a journey

Starting from the depths of a blazing torch

Ending in a tranquil forest

Where the birds harmonize like an army cheering after a successful battle

Where the tree's beauteous green embraces visitors with a motherly whisper

Where the wind reassures that enemies will fly by

The journey is still dotted with eruptions

Dust is in the air

I dust off my eyes

Climb through the rubble

REM

Growing

The cracks on my shelf

My fantasies

Lying

To the elves on the street

Good REM sleep

Destroying

The fantasies on the wheel

Nocks are at my window

AMBER SKY

Stars are lit by the glow of my fire

The orange flame dances with the night's dazzling diamonds

I witness the stunning and joyous motion

Without happiness feeling any devotion

Flying through the praise

No one thinks there is a maze

I do

I do

Flames keep dancing with the diamonds in the night sky

Everyone says the motion is heavenly

Too heavy

Too much nothing

There is something

Will you walk with me to my home?

I want to be alone

HALLELUJAH

I almost lost her cherry sweet soul

In a titanic collision of metal and gears

I almost lost her soothing voice

Originating from the sun's warm rays

I almost lost her

But she's alive and well

A divine force repelled the metal and gears with its thunderous voices

And spiritual prowess

I am eternally grateful that she has been saved

She's alive and well

Hallelujah

I shall sing

THE VOICE

I found my way to the front of the crowd

Strings are plucked

Movement drives the flow

I thought I found peace

I thought I had found the proper way to bleed

Struggles left the center of the stage

Struggles released by a voice with a rage

Will these struggles turn this burnt page?

Not for me

Not for me

Blood in my brain started boiling

Struggles from voices didn't help me breath that night

Over and over I remembered how your beautiful smile tore my limbs

I hate you

OCEAN

This game is too insane for our domain

Join me on the ocean

I'll show you where beauty is tamed

We'll reach for the sun on the brightest mornings

Build barriers from the waves and their grasp

But the look in your eye will never collapse

Your sword will remain sharp and fast

We've arrived

STARE

I still see your smile in my sleep

Gorgeous eyes

They glow and repeat

Hair a lot messier

A stare beaten down by questions

A call for my attention to release my confessions

Rejection from a gold laced heart leaves deep wounds

Healed

But my blood hasn't forgotten

CAN I GO HOME?

I can't have

My own head

My own real life

It's been taken

Don't you try to say I'm insane

Don't you try to say I'm sane

I don't want to know if I'm either one

Can I ask a question?

Am I done?

OBSERVING THE TOWN

Greenish love in your basement

And so much more

Dangerous wings flying around your town

I don't know what you're doing

But I know your summer sound

The masters of the supply are waiting for a different kind of green

You can stay here for your mental eternity

My pen is composing lyrics

Memories playing songs with destinies inside

You write with a different pen

You're giving me some clues

I'll follow your dark tracks

By the time of midnight

They will find you

They're watching you

You're luxury

Is the most fragile secret you've ever held

LOVELY HEART

Are you suffering?

Are heated regrets boiling in your throat?

When my commitment to you only meets loneliness

My fingers will write with the moisture from your tears

I'll write on the cold brick wall

Rage is a universe

Galaxies of decisions

Born from destructive beginnings

A lovely heart is a snake

Treat the slithery creature with love

The snake will shine with mesmerizing scales

Treat the slithery creature with abandonment

The snake will slither into your joy and strike!

NEVER

I will never bother you

My laughter will never reach your ears

I will trap my words in the ground

No sound

No sound

You know you're right

There are flowers held by a black hood

The flowers are placed on the dirt

Silence

Silence

The hood is now one with the soul

The hood won't know where to go

HAUNT ME

I tell you time and time again

I know the way they talk

The fingerprints on your handprint will wash away

Right on the lock

I know the dirty glares

Violent staring

We're not spared

We know you read me like a book

But the chapters aren't fully there

If I was meant to be scarred that's all I need to know

Siren songs can be found everywhere

So, beware

Love under skies of fall

Next winter was the worst of all

See yah in the next five weeks

Maybe this time I won't be so alone

HYBRID VIGOR

The clash of two hands

Loving or mad

Strays away from fleeing the scene

The hands stay

Locked in place

Either in the presence of love

Or the presence of rage

A concoction is born

Two breeds in one

Don't deny our mysteries

We're two enigmas in one

We can't erase our marks

We can't erase our breed

We can't leave this scene

Accept this

We must

TREMBLE

The scarlet runs down my fangs like oil

I figure such a sight wouldn't even let you tremble

I fought hard for my scars

What do I stand for?

I'm a puppet without strings

A dagger without a course

Let me taste your stories

Maybe it'll be my lethal dose

LOCK

Do you want to riot down the street?

With your hands groping a sword?

Do you want to scream on the tele?

I see you wrote a handy anthem

Do you desire to bury voices?

In piles of oinks from a War Pig's snout?

Then leave my humble home

Lock the door on your way out

GRASS

Welcome to my grave

There's no turning back

Stones for miles and miles

The grass towers past our trees

How will you ever leave?

TATTOO

She'll declare the love in the air

My woman, my curse, my mark I shall bear

A tattoo to devotion to precautions

The ink scorching my

Tongue

Lips

Fingers

Cheeks

I'm devoid of healthy flesh

A burnt meal on a plate

She eats me like mysteries

She inhales me like air

CHOIR

November sunshine is few and far between

Tattoos on bathroom walls

A faded sympathy

The Killing Joke sneers at our pride

All the mountains impose a shadow down below

This darkened choir

Sings to and fro

HOLIDAY

Lovers sleep upon the death of urgent sight

Warning signs don't matter

They burn in the October romance

Fall embers fool the eyes

Don't let you see the lies

Only dying gold can be seen falling from the branches

Beware upcoming outcomes of blind holiday love

Lovers snap the warnings raining upon conjoined lips

They kill their urgent sight

They all burn in the holiday romance

PINOCCHIOS

Leaders fly to and fro

Valued greens in their pockets

Trophies from their day of guiding sheep

Donkey ears grow on our high seated pinocchios

Our crickets have been sliced

Diced

And served to the highest bidder

EYES

Insanity is a funny gesture

From the brain to the eyes

I see the sky in a different shade than the fellow with no pen

Not all faces desire to be drawn

Not all crimes desire to be remembered

Pens don't take requests

Pens take victims

To the stories behind my days

MIRROR

I look in the mirror of my cell

This is not a prison

Nor protection

Just an image far from her hand

She knows not of my mirrors

But only my laughs

"Ha ha" I draw in my notebook

Don't worry, I'm just here with the glass

TIRED, HAPPIER, WORKING

Tired

Happier

Working

Shouting less

Staring

More pain

More bandages

Spent less money today

Wore less black today

Got in a fight

Started shaking

Remembered medication

Tired

Happier

Working

Tired

Happier

Working

Tired

Happier

Working

Don't Wake Up

Have you ever slept in the whispering wind?

The pale moonlight dancing in your head

Don't wake up, don't stop dreaming

We're all around you

We're always here

You don't want to wake

Wars pass by

Turn a blind eye

Pain will pass you by

CLOWNS

The clowns laugh

Clowns march

Clowns perform all day and night

Us, the clowns, brand our smiles onto your grin

The heat of your screams satisfied all our needs

You all will listen

You all will pay attention

We'll send in the clowns

Brand our smiles on your leaders

STORY

Stories don't snuggle your palm like a lover

They lick your imagination

With saliva like gas for the aging vehicle

Our minds are older

Peeling like dead skin

The aging can't be stopped

But it can be moisturized

HOW DO I TELL HER I WANNA HOLD HER HAND?

She always had a knack for depleting my sentences to mere dust in the wind

You would think a poet would have plenty to announce

On a regular day I would possess valleys upon valleys of words to herd out of my

mouth like cattle

But this wasn't one of those days

The browns of her eyes deepened like canyons

The kind an explorer wants to get dangerously lost in

But never desire to be set free

The curls of her hair are like a summer evening

Where the sunshine upon a mountain of lush, gleaming soil

Injects fantasies of growth and prosperity into an admirer's subconscious

Her beauty almost haunts me

59

An image fried into my brain

Her presence so close

Her love so far away

I know she'll never desire these words

But alas, my pen writes on

I'm a lost handyman

Always constructing words

For an audience turned away

DIARY

The train arrives at my station

A vehicle

Black as a crow

Black as my required attire

I enter the mouth of the crow

The morning's events still in my heart

Like a dagger with a singular course...

Inside

An empty seat seems welcoming

Isolation seems heartwarming

A book whispers a scream

Like a banshee with no one to scare

Isolation is needed

But curiosity is pulling

I open the book

Within seconds I gasp

Flipping through the pages of a forgotten past

Oh, how I miss him

Oh, how I loved him

A flood falls on my skirt as daggers pierce my eyes to leak my immortal regrets

Now his memories are just words

Now his voice is trapped in ink

I saw his stone in the yard today

I saw his stone in the yard today

BLACK PORTRAIT

Wait a minute cause the tide is turning

On a beach filled with portraits and sand

He never thought a black frame would reach her fragile hands

The hood was put on

The flowers dying from the weight of her silent atmosphere

Trees have grown here

A maze is taunting

Young but quiet

Determined but hollow

She turns back

The road home is far

However

She remembers

The black frame

A last memory is remembered

Of her

And his forest

LIES

I've been a fool to gaze into the sky with a grin

Not much people can be trusted

No surprise to me

Hienas with Sanchos are very common to see

Sancho walks with an innocent smirk

A boy's hiena in his arms

Grooming his prickly conscious

Feeling his silky hair

Dreaming of his strawberry sweet kiss

Non-stop talk of his dazzling glamor

Lies slither through straight faces

Or maybe they weren't lies

Maybe she's more idiotic than I realized

Anger held in

Anger twisted like limbs

Refusal to admit the truth

A fire summoned

Sancho still smiles

Sancho knows he'll win

I've been a fool to gaze into the sky with a grin

Not much people can be trusted

No surprise to me

Hienas with Sanchos are very common to see

GRAY

Keep the lights off

Surroundings seep gray

Walls keep my glance

Small breaths are the maximum sound

Won't dare to sleep

Won't dare to grin

Ain't this fun?

BIG BLACK DOORS

Looks below

At the dirt on the ground

Feels quite superior

He's a man on the moon

But don't be fooled

Behind big black doors

He's an ant in the ground

Who lives with no sound

Except the man

That lives in his ears

Don't listen to him

Or you can handshake your fears

BLACKEST FLAMES

Today's sun is darker

Shadows rip the skies

Rain is running smoothly

Across the beautiful lies

Our forest grew inside here

We fed it with both our hands

But you stopped caring for it

You were blind to the black flames

Our forest is gone

Burned to the ground

We left the last tree

We didn't make a sound

The last plant

It fell and met the rust

No one was around

To hear it fall

In the black desert of dust

PSYCHOLOGY

flawless figures and tricks

That don't work with your psychology of conversation

Do your words mean 4, 5 warnings or more?

The sunset is laid to rest on your skin

Secrets and distance

The riddles we were subjected to

My music played to the moon

All my lovely tricks

Feelings and creeks

Didn't fit with the psychology of conversation

Your illumination

My creations

Love is a wave we feel

Spreading its tides properly is a lesson we learn

After much time of swimming vigorously

And floating angrily

GET OUT

Look how sunken in the children sit

How our papers weep at the mere contact of ink

Dark like our mortal hearts

The teacher's no bother

She just stares passively through our sunken figure

Because we don't sleep

There's no time for that weakness

That mortal vulnerability

No time for loving lips to slide down our skin

That would require confidence in secrets

A self-esteem we're not permitted to utter

Not in these walls

Not ever

MOONLIGHT

I've always hated the public eye, today was no different. The waiter asked for

my order, I graciously gave it to him: a bacon cheeseburger, cooked medium

well, cheddar cheese, and no tomatoes or pickles. This was all I wanted, the

only substance in existence I desired to consume at that very moment. The

social interaction should've ended there, but alas, my greatest fear decided to

materialize itself. I tried to hide my twitch with every murderous ounce of

strength I learned to build up over the years, but the body had other interests

My head rolled on my neck like a barrel of rotten wine. A slight squawk

escaped my lips like a herd of dying geese. The waiter laughed, pathetically

covering his mouth with his bony hand. My choices were then realized, I

knew what had to be done.

I got up from my seat, walked over to the waiter, and put my hand on his

shoulder. The man was understandably confused. There was no way for him

to know my intentions, at least, not yet. I asked the man if he's ever gazed upon the moonlight with bloodshot eyes, the waiter shook his head. That's when I unfolded my plan for his fate. My fist sucker punched both his eyes. The man fell to the ground in agonizing pain and disbelief. The rest of the customers screamed in dismay, one of them even called the police. The waiter got up from the floor, recovering from the pain. I couldn't stand his determination to defy my obvious authority in this standoff. This mere man thinks he can get up after having his body in contact with the floor? Where dirty shoes rain masses of bacteria on every inch of the surface area below? Disgusting! I threw a wine bottle over his head like a lethal baseball bat. The slicing of his skin and fountain of blood exploding out of the area of impact was like a masterfully structured renaissance painting. I smiled as the blood covered my face like romantic rain in a cheesy movie. I giggled in the midst of his screeching and bawling on the floor, it was just so orgasmic. The high remained while I examined the little man's body slowly slipping away forever. He got what he deserved.

I had the time of my life.

The police carried me away into their vehicles of imprisonment. I looked

forward to my future endeavors. Perhaps prison will have plenty more bodies

to examine, new blood to be spilt. Until then, I hope you enjoyed the story of

my happiest moment. The description of the most beautiful day.

CHRISTMAS NIGHT

Our Christmas jingle shall be heard through the hills

Up the mountains

Through the skies

To be known by all creatures

Emmanuel's joyful bliss shall ignite our holy hymns

And Christmas trees

Like a mighty fire

On a towering castle

Presented for us mere humans

On Christmas night

DECADENCE

The embodiments of human decadence

Enlists themselves into many wars

Whichever side is chosen will be decided by brutal circumstance

Of surviving blood sucking winter

Or drifting through bodies killed by empty success

ANGELICALLY WOVEN

Is romance meant to be rekindled after absence?

Does her desire for a lover include my hands?

My eyes?

My lips?

I've been made aware of her pain

Like a warrior comforting a deep wound

I wish I could bend her reality like clay

Into a mold of purely lovely embraces

Why anyone would hurt a soul woven by angel hair and painted with heavenly tears

I do not know

And frankly

I do not wish to understand

MY LOVE

Your wonderous image gets foggier every day. I can no longer remember the browns of your eyes… the curves of your smile. I have photos, but alas, they are mere glorified memorabilia of times emotionally observed.

I am unaware of where your beauty has taken its course on the flying carpet of time. Where do your eyes shine during moments of outward joy? Does your hair still curl like dazzling spiral galaxies? Or have your luscious locks reached for something different?

I can't recall or account for any past journey where I've discovered beauty such as yours. I can't even fathom allowing myself to admire our old photos, they don't represent your growth in our spinning top of a homeland. My goal is to perfectly capture your ever-growing self in a memory everlasting. It'll follow us in the crater we'll leave in the concept of memories, because what's the true goal of remembering your beauty with a strategy of fading into blankness?

PURPLE HEART

Hallways are lined with purple hearts

In the classroom
A fire is seized
In the hallways
A society takes flight
But there is never control in the darkness or light

Political admiration dictates the flow of psychological cooperation

The hallway is lined with purple hearts
Dark bruises blacken the curious autopsies
While hallway regulars target the weak to drown their accused disease to the seas

Purple hearts are awarded here
The ceremony waterboards us forever

BLANK

Blank

Wet

Humid

Thoughtless

Is my mind in this jungle of desire

I have nothing to put down onto my paper skin

My digital face

Unfortunate

Horrible

DRAGON ON THE SEA

Admiral Yi

Hero of the land

Naval force with the shell of a turtle

Fire in the eyes of his men

The red liquid of life bursting from enemy wounds

Carnage in the waters of Korea

Death inflicted to reach the goal

The certainty of victory

Awarded to Admiral Yi

CRICKETS SING

Crickets Sing

Videos play

TV's chatter

Drinks splatter

Feet clutter

Voices tower

Laughs share

Hands hold

LOST

The bird's song is not meant for us

Neither the king cats of the savannah

Or the surviving beasts of the forest's maze

They're too busy trudging through the vast array of scars Death has left on their pav

Gnashing at the meat of their breasts

Digging its claws into the piles of frozen tears

Lost in the skin cracking cold

RIDDLE PART 2

Part 1 resides in *Red Velvet*

Todd was ready for hell.

The police had been attempting for weeks to get information out of the attempted murderer. The good cop/bad cop routine only got laughs out of Todd's rotten, black teeth. He didn't know why he should care about his fate, he had nothing to lose at this point. Some interrogations resulted in Todd being turned into a life size, bloody rag doll; but it didn't matter. His palms were stitched to the brim and his left knee was also stitched beyond comprehension. There wasn't any way the pain of injury and capture could get any worse, especially since that lying witch is still alive. Cheryl's father had a plan to take care of their little obstacle, but did it have to take so long?

While Cheryl and Danny were healing in the hospital, Todd was planning his escape. His injuries might prohibit his plan from being effective, but no matter. Pure human brutality seemed like enough to rip open the skull of an unsuspecting guard. An example needed to be made of ANYONE who thought they could lock up a higher being such as Todd. For now, however, he decided to wait. The perfect opportunity will arise itself in a matter of time

"HEY!"

Todd looked up from his pitiful excuse for a bed. He enjoyed his moments of silent monologuing almost as much as slipping cold metal through warm, wet flesh. Oh yes, very wet, sweaty, screaming flesh.

"LOOK AT ME, INMATE!"

A guard was looking down at Todd. The man wore a black policeman uniform and eyes fueled by pure disgust. Todd had seen those eyes before; he didn't like that.

Not.

One.

Bit.

You're supposed to be in the cafeteria eating! I guess we have to keep scum ke you alive for some damn reason!" the officer shouted. "Everyone else has left and you're still in your fucking cell! What the hell is wrong with you!"

odd looked around at the empty jail cells, chuckled for a bit, and got up from is mattress to be walked to the cafeteria. He was only two feet out of his cell when he decided to mutter something he's been dying to say.

"Hey officer" Todd chuckled.

"What the fuck is it, inmate?"

odd chuckled some more. His laugh struck too much fear to allow the officer ɔ reach for his gun. It sounded like a mix between an ape's dying moan and a hyena's threatening growl. The laugh then ended abruptly, almost out of nowhere. What was left of the murderous joy remained a flame stemming from a hellish rage.

"Are you aware of why I'm in this jail in the first place?"

"Yeah, cause you allegedly tortured, brutally hurt, and traumatized two your teens. You monster! NOW KEEP MOVING!"

The policeman aggressively pushed Todd forward. After a couple of minute of walking the two of them had almost reached the door at the end of the hallway.

"Officer, what I want to tell you…is that one of my victims was a young girl… an ex of mine… and guess what?"

"You better shut the fuck up, inmate"

Todd looked straight into the guard's eyes. His smile widened, his eyes contained a grey stillness. Todd's black, rotting gums reeked of diseased fles alongside his cut up, bloody cheeks. The officer grabbed his gun but dropped it when Todd stepped towards him.

"She liked it"

"What the hell?" The officer muttered.

"She fuckin liked it"

94

"SHUT UP!" The officer screeched.

'odd grabbed the officer's face, stroking his cheek and placing his other hand on the man's left eye.

"And you will too"

"AAAAAHHHHHHH"

Danny knew fear had strangled his tongue into submission. Attempting to form a sentence was like putting a hand on a hot stove. How does someone reply to such a bold statement? Did Danny even desire a response? Was Cheryl's father connected to Todd's violent lunacy? Was the violence not ver? Danny assumed he was safe in this hospital room; not even Todd would be crazy enough to attack him here. At least, that's what Danny hoped.

Cheryl's father had been awaiting a response from Danny, but nothing was muttered. Danny didn't know of the realities about to be revealed to him, thrown upon him and his dear lover.

"Wha- what do you mean?" Danny asked with slight bits of sweat flowing down his forehead. Cheryl's father was relieved that one of them broke the dreadfully awkward silence. After all, a young boy can't squeal without curiosity latching around his every nerve.

"Danny, oh Danny. I knew my daughter was cheating on Todd with you for months."

"What does that have to do with anything, old man?" Danny asked. His sweat was increasing, his skin cringed at the cold touch of the fluid. Danny's hands were clenching his seat's armrests with unrelenting force, but no pain was felt. Danny's hyper focus on the man in front of him wouldn't allow for mere pain to distract his mind.

Cheryl's father raised up one finger into the air while his body stood calm like an evening breeze. "You didn't let me finish my sentence" he said.

A doctor ran into the room, interrupting Cheryl's father. She was breathing heavily and holding her chest. A trail of crimson colored liquid had followed her through the hallway. She tried to mutter words but fell to the floor in a ide puddle of blood. Danny knew what this meant, Danny was not prepared. He looked up at Cheryl's father to see him smiling. Danny shot up from his seat, dropping his automotive magazine.

"WHY ARE YOU SMILING? HE'S HERE! TODD'S FUCKING HERE! AAHH!"

'heryl's father had knocked out Danny with one sucker punch to the head. He then pulled out a pocketknife and started carving Danny's face. Blood splattered, surrounding his stabbed, carved, and deceased body. Cheryl's 'ather loved the masterpiece he was unfolding for Todd to see. It was worthy of an exhibit. Cheryl watched this all happen.

And she did nothing.

Nothing but shake in her bed.

Staring.

And pathetically weeping.

97

Todd, after massacring many hospital workers, made his way to Cheryl's hospital room. He had gotten a tip to where it was from strangling it out of a little boy who had given Cheryl balloons the other day. The little boy's body was laid down amongst other bodies of patients and doctors. Todd walked into Cheryl's room to find Danny nailed to the bed with the words "Liar, Cheater, Pants on Fire" written in blood on his shirt. Danny's face had horizontal stripes carved into his face with blood flowing down from the wounds.

"Why the stripes?" Todd asked.

"I don't know... it just felt... right" Cheryl's father explained.

There was a moment of silence between the two. Todd couldn't believe the fun was over. This journey would come to a close after today. All Todd could feel was disturbing, parasitic, self-loathing. He hoped Cheryl was still alive for one last date.

"So, I trust you held up your end of the bargain?"

Cheryl's father went behind a closet and pulled out his daughter. She was bloody, beaten, and crying out rivers. She continually punched her father in the face, but to no avail. She was weak, she was defeated. Cheryl's father threw her into Todd's excited and giddy arms. He embraced her panicking and crying body with much, much joy.

"GET OFF OF ME! GET AWAY! AAAAAAHHHHH!"

QUIET!" Todd screamed while holding Cheryl's neck. "We're going to have lots of fun in my basement. Lots of bloody, painful, fun."

"AAAAHHHHHHHH!"

Cheryl couldn't stop crying, no matter how hard she tried to remain strong. Todd started carrying her out of the hospital while Cheryl's father waved goodbye with a bright, plastic smile.

And away Cheryl and Todd went.

Gone, gone, gone.

Gone, gone, gone.

HORROR

'Twas a night most dreary

Scorned with pity

Where the foxes lay resting

Thou shall not question

The white gore of the midnight striking clock

The blue blood of an empty dock

Don't question the horrors

You will regret the cursed curiosity

THE DREAM

A beauteous dream inserted itself into my midnight slumber

Sent my heart aflutter and awoke me to a restless reality

I don't think I can take another dose of that mystical foolery

We strolled through the brick castle hallways

Gazing upon the countryside of fertile green allure

"A happy year we've shared,

My beloved"

was the sentence whispered through your lip's pearly glow

My dreamlike manifestation believed your stories

But I awoke

To the silence

To the darkness

Can you find it in your soul to believe what I have seen?

Can you find it in your heart to listen?

I CARE

Long dark hair

Release your hurt into my embrace

I am here for you

Like a sweet metaphor for a shed tear

You already read my pain like encrypted hieroglyphs

Yes, I gave you the key

Now give me yours

I want to cleanse your scars through a baptism of joy

I pray that I'll be able to achieve such a task

Don't hurt yourself

Long dark hair

LONG DARK HAIR PART 2

Dear long dark hair

With streaks of blonde like gold erupting from the Earth's crust

Through a volcano of dust spouting out a beauty that'll never rust

I'll wait for you

Dear long dark hair

You're not ready for your gold to be loved

You have every right to reject my silver

But I still feel a sliver of feeling

That in time our treasures will join

105

In the sunset of Denver nights

Where the sky turns rose quartz

Where I'll wait for you

I hope you'll wait for me too

Because my diamonds belong to you

SPIDER

The spiders on the floor

Crawl up my sleeping stone self

I have no intention to stop them

I'm comfortable right here

Where the elements tear me away like butter

I'm nourishment for the dirt

Food for our creatures

As goes life and death

To dust I shall return

GEMS

I hate the way you speak

To the knives impaling my hands

Pretty burgundy dripping down your skirt

The little boy's favorite color

You sliced my guards

Awoken my cell

Leave me, enchantress!

Leave me, witch!

I've had enough of your lapis lazuli coated lips

Your malachite flavored skin

Leave me be

In my cave of my own gems

Made in the USA
Middletown, DE
18 July 2023

34851554R00071